The Melancholy Chronicles:

A Collection of Short Stories and Poems.

By Hunter Blaise

2021

For my grandmother who never thought

my dreams were too crazy to achieve.

"And heavy on the rum"

Table of contents

The world is art 7

The shot that rebounded 14

The white room 33

X 42

A princely Character 47

Carrollwood 51

To my ignorance 62

A second chance 70

How criminal 74

A best friend 77

Ghosted 84

Grandma's house 91

Poems

Cold showers 109

What is tomorrow 112

Until we meet again 115

The moon cries 118

A broken oven 121

If only she knew 124

Freedom 127

The garden 130

Vows 133

To my grandmother 138

Quotations 141

A note from the author 143

The World is Art

The whole world is a painting. Strokes run horizontal and vertical, while colors are vivid or pastel. The sky cradles the Earth in hopes those down on it feel a sense of happiness when that striking blue turns into a spring day's paint pallet. Although, not everyone can see these paintings.

If you asked me what a smartphone looked like, I sadly could not answer. When I was a little girl I remember touching flip phones and tape recorders, but the memory as to what they looked like, vanished. Many pity my sight, and others dare not mention it. The world isn't just beautiful in sight though.

When I lost my eyesight, it was a devastating and trying time. My eyes didn't blow out like a light bulb though, it was a process -- a slow and terrifying one. I was afraid to fall asleep every night because I knew when I woke up the posters in my room would be more blurry and my photos have no faces. Simple tasks such as crossing the street turned into a test of survival. I couldn't see the cars, and they couldn't see me.

    A few summers ago, I met a man -- he was unlike anything else in my life. He took care of me in ways I didn't know a human could for another. When I told him I was going to go blind someday, that didn't matter to him. He promised to take care of me no matter what. It wasn't his words that brought me to tears that day, it was the realization I would wake up and never see his beautiful face again.

    Some nights when the power would go out I panicked and cried because I thought it was happening, I thought I finally lost it all. My love would hold me tight and reassure me he couldn't see either in the blackout. Someday eventually became a reality though. I woke up like I always did, and again, nothing. I was calm because I figured it was another power outage… but the lights never came on. Crying and screaming, I couldn't compose myself. I couldn't fathom that the day actually came. My love held my face in his hands and said "Look at me, what's wrong, why are you crying". That was the issue though. I couldn't look at him, I couldn't look at anyone, or anything. With a moment of silence, he knew that day came too.

I couldn't hear him crying, but I felt his warm tears travel between the creases of my hands when I reached for his face. It was a warmth I never felt before.

    Adjusting was hard, but to this day I still feel it was harder for my husband. Simple tasks turned into assignments. He helped me scrub the places I missed in the shower and quietly would fix my dresses when they piled up. We weren't wealthy, or poor, we were content. He guides me not only in the world around us but to help me find the best version of myself.

    Who could ever say they enjoy being blind, but even so I can't say I'm miserable either. The beauty of living is finding new ways to be happy when unexpected things happen.

The whole world is a painting. Strokes run horizontal and vertical, while colors are vivid or pastel. The sky cradles the earth in hopes those down on it feel a sense of happiness when that striking blue turns into a spring day's paint pallet. I find my peace in music, taking in the scents and textures of the world. I thought I knew it all when I had sight since we believe that is the only way to enjoy something, how I was wrong. There is an undiscovered world that my other senses have yet to indulge. Of course, I could sit around withering away as life flashes by with my resentment of how things ended up for me, but eyesight has no control over how well my life could be. I now hear, touch, and feel the world for how it truly is, and to some that's a scary way to live. No one believes me when I tell them about my beautiful life, but it's not one I see.

        It's one I feel.

A Shot That Rebounded

I should have seen it coming, but how could anyone see it coming? I just loved her so much but maybe my ignorance made me blind to the red flags presented to me. I wasn't stabbed, or mugged, or even killed. It was something much worse, something so criminal I'm shaking trying to say it. I was cheated on. Which if you ask me is astronomically worse than all three of those things mentioned above combined.

I was a Freshman trying to blend into the crowd, ya know the cool kids and all. In this journey of teenage acceptance I met these two guys during lunch hour who promised they would make my highschool years *thrilling*.. whatever that meant. I took them up on the offer because they were Sophomores and I thought it'd be good for my reputation. One of the guys, by the name of Daniel, reminded me a lot of myself actually. He was reserved and polite but still gave off that cool guy vibe. Then there was Allen. This guy was a total badass from top of his choppy buzz cut to the steel on the tips of his father's boots. He was also like me… well future me at least. As some months went on I started to realize all the trouble Allen would get us into but he wasn't wrong, highschool did become *thrilling*.

Winter break was approaching and since we live in the hellish sun beat state of Florida, winter break was really just a mini summer vacation. Even so, us Floridians like to believe we have some sort of winter when we hang those fake icicles off the house or wear boots like our feet aren't in a dutch oven. I spend every year in my knit snowman sweater eager to open up presents. Of course Santa isn't real but when your life is so bleak at least it adds some type of magic. This *was* the tradition until Allen totally fucked everything up. That ass apparently told my mom his parents invited me to stay at their beach house for the break, which we all know is such bullshit, and my mom said "it would be such a great time!", she let her baby boy go off with this questionable character for winter break. You might be asking yourself why I didn't just say no, well I'm not going to say peer pressure because I'm scared of Allen or anything but let's just say you never say no to Allen if you want your limbs intact. So there I was, packing my suitcase to go who knows where to spend my Christmas that Santa would probably frown on.

  Okay so it wasn't total bullshit Allen's parents did have a beach house and we were allowed to stay there...sorta. To be frank, Allen was kicked out for god knows what and they sent him there. Why he wanted me and Daniel to come along, who the hell knows. Since Allen was the only one who knew how to drive we were essentially at his mercy. He pulled up to my house in this admittingly really nice van and I threw my suitcase in the backseat and scootched on next to Daniel who already looked beat. As if my plans didn't change enough he tells us there's a few more people tagging along. I glanced over at Daniel who looked un-surprised as I tried to compose myself from actually shitting my pants over this. Who were these guys? What if they're Seniors? Or worse, college students? Are they gonna be nice to a pussy like me? We pull up to this average, yet cute house and we must have waited about ten minutes. I remember Allen muttering "da fucks takin so long" under his breath tapping on the wheel. The door opened, out came these two tiny giggling, very pink, girls..? They weren't just girls, they were hot girls! Daniel got out to open the trunk for them so they could put their bags in. One of the girls with a short brown bob and big blue eyes scooted in next to me as the blonde girl sat up front with Allen. Daniel closed the trunk and sat on the end, leaving me squished against this adorable human being. I discovered the blonde girl's name was Natalie, simply because her and Allen wouldn't shut the fuck up. Seriously, who needs a radio when you have those two. If he wasn't driving they'd definitely be three sessions in if you catch my drift. Anyways, at that point I still had no idea who was sitting next to me until "So…. I believe we go to the same school?" Wait, these girls are from our school? Am I really that oblivious? Nervous I turned to her and replied with "Ahhh yeah! Just started this year" with an odd noise at the end that honestly I couldn't tell you. To my surprise she giggled and told me she started this year as well! Another Freshman? Is it my lucky day? How on earth did she get wrapped up with Allen? Once we started talking we couldn't stop.

She liked biology, I liked biology, she enjoyed swimming, *I* enjoyed swimming, you get the picture. This girl turned a three-hour drive into ten minutes. The best part was, I found out her name is Samantha.

    When we got to the beach house it was actually quite nice to say the least. It was definitely a house on the beach and well what more could you ask for. As Daniel and I were unloading the car, I asked him more about Samantha to see if maybe he knew where she came from. He admitted he didn't know much about her aside that her ex-Boyfriend Derek used to be best friends with Allen. At the time I shrugged of it, everyone has an ex...well, except me that year. I figured she wouldn't talk about him because it would be too painful and I didn't want to ruin a relationship before it began. The three days we were there I got close to Samantha, it was a feeling I never had before actually. I had friends but in the short time getting to know her it just felt like no one understood me quite like she did. Our last night there all five of us went to the shore to watch the fireworks, man Miami knows how to party but that's a whole other story. I did something I never did before out of pure passion and hope, I grabbed Samantha's hand. Nothing more, nothing less, but feeling her hand in mine evoked a new emotion for me. She gently folded her little fingers on my hand and the tense feeling I had before vanished as I just inhaled the new world around me. After the last firework struck, and it was just us in the peaceful darkness showered in the light of the moon, I turned to her. "Will you be my girlfriend?"

"Yes."

    From that moment on I couldn't tell you a day we weren't together. I would wait by the school gate to walk her home everyday and everyday just felt like I fell in love with her all over again because she was just that amazing. My relationship with Daniel and Allen began to drift, mostly because they were older than me and a year does a lot to mature a person. We spoke from time to time but I didn't want to be the cool guy anymore, I just wanted to be happy with Samantha. She brought magic to my life, like a totally new level of magic, that not even Santa could bring. When it was just me and her I felt like I could conquer the world. There was something about Samantha though that often would worry me. She struggled with severe depressive episodes. If I could transfer her pain to me if it meant she would feel better, I would but I can't begin to believe that I understand what she goes through. Due to this, there were times where she wasn't her usual chipper self, times where she would come over and not say a word, just curl up in my lap and close her eyes. Times where her hair was so knotted the comb stuck but without judgment I always detangled it. Times where she whispered to me she wanted to kill herself but was too afraid. I felt useless that I couldn't make her want to live. How do you make someone *want* to live? The world liked to tell me it was puppy love, but my age did not change the fact that I loved her and wanted her to be the best version of herself.

    We were Juniors now, how fast time flies when you're in love, at least I was that is. Things began to drift but not on my end. There were days she walked right past me without a word and I took it as she needed space. Weeks between replies when I asked her how she was feeling. Since we weren't in any classes together, I didn't get to see her much except for lunch. On the days she decided to actually sit with me, she would just put her head down and not say a word. I never got upset since I knew there was so much on her plate that it was bending. During the summer of Sophomore year her friend passed away and she never really was the same after that. I often felt guilty because I don't handle death well and maybe I wasn't the support she needed at the time. Then it happened, the week before spring break she disappeared. She wasn't at school, I couldn't get through to her by phone, and her parents turned me away when I tried to visit. Spring break came and went and still no word where she went. My heart sank when I sent her a message on Facebook and the "sorry this message cannot be delivered" binged. She blocked me, but why. I was starting to understand depression a little better as I felt myself slipping, the only difference is I now have no one.

    I asked Daniel if we could meet up at the food court in the mall, and with no questions asked he said yes. This was a

Daniel type of situation because he is so calm. We grabbed some Taco bell and camped out at a table that probably hasn't been cleaned in a week, but yet it was comforting to just sit there and do close to nothing. I told Daniel the whole situation and apologized for pushing him and Allen out. Like the saint he was he reassured me there was no bad blood. I looked up at him and smiled, but it was quickly wiped off my face when I saw her. It was Samantha in a group of people I didn't know. I went to jolt up to run to her but my feet were glued to the floor when a passing man walked by and that's when I saw it. She was holding hands with another guy. I don't know if I saw red before or after I gasped for air. As I tensed up I felt myself about to run over as Daniel grabbed my arm. Ever so quiet he mumbled "That's Derek". My heart felt through my chest and onto the floor. If you didn't think that was enough of a slap, Allen was with them too. After a deep dreadful breath I marched over there and wiped the smile off her face too. She had the nerve to hide behind Derek's arm. All I remember screaming is "What the fuck" on the top of my lungs. Daniel put his hand on my shoulder to try and calm me down. Trying not to cry in front of those losers I turned my back and sat down to finish my pathetic bean burrito. Everything was blurry but one figure came into clarity as they sat down in front of me. It was Samantha. I found out that she apparently transferred schools and in that transition she realized how much she missed Derek and how they were a better fit together. I felt myself laughing under my breath because it was so stupid, it was all so stupid. She told me she didn't want to hurt my feelings but was too scared to talk to me. I was baffled and told her that not telling me not only pissed me off but not my feelings are beyond hurt. Tears started rolling down her face as she whispered "I'm so sorry". Without a word in reply I got up and gave her a short yet firm hug since I knew this would probably be the last time I see her. I watched her get up and walk into the horizon with that moron, and this was it, I never saw Samantha again.

A few months since then passed and to my enjoyment I finally found out why Derek was an ex in the first place -- he cheated on her! And, surprise surprise, he cheated on her again. As much as I wanted to laugh, I couldn't bring myself to it as I felt bad for her in a strange way. It's amazing how lack of communication impacts a relationship. Had she told me her intentions,

she never would've needed to cheat.

The White Room

This story contains graphic nature.

It was a beautiful little room. The walls splashed with colors every which way within this little room. The copper wooden panels ran wall to wall. The floor with different rugs scattered across the chestnut playplace as if placed there by accident. The room had many shelves, they held toys and trinkets as far as the eye could see but only few could see them.

There were plenty of dolls in her room which had beautiful big blue eyes just like the girl who pondered there. All the furniture was white; a bed with trillions of stuffed animals, a desk which had no purpose, and a little night stand that held a bright pink pair of sunglasses and some bracelets. The room also had a white coat hanger with little jackets and decorative canes which were also white. This beautiful little room belonged to the even littler girl by the name of Elle.

Elle was the age of seven and spent many hours in her room, which who wouldn't be proud of owning. Every morning she'd walk to her coat hanger to grab what she needed and started her day just to put everything back in the afternoon. Now, Elle unlike most girls her age didn't have much to do. She could play, or she could dance, but she preferred not to due to the fear of failing.

Elle calmed her mind by laying on her favorite rug, one of many that was scattered, and listened to music. The music was like an explosion of excitement in her mind. She always tried not to listen to too much in fear that the words will overwhelm her imagination.

Her mother often would listen to the music with her and describe what the lyrics may mean. This beautiful little room had many tall mirrors as well, but Elle never bothered to look into any of them, not once. Now Elle didn't have many friends other than her mom. That was alright though, since she always worried about someone messing with her room behind her back. Elle was always upset when she had to leave her room. When she walked toward the door, it was always as if the rugs were grabbing at her little toes begging her not to leave, as if the room feared for her. When Elle had left the room it stood still and waited for her return. The walls were still colorful and each doll and trinket remained in place waiting to see her again. It was as if the room came alive when she walked through the door, because that beautiful little room did its best to see her smile.

As Elle grew up, many dolls were knocked into and shattered on the floor and many rugs dragged so far they could never be found again. Elle would cry and cry because she wished she wasn't so clumsy. After her mother came in to help her clean the mess, her room restored it's beautiful nature once more. Elle was now twelve and growing up she had to deal with more responsibility. Music didn't help her much anymore but she slowly became fond of reading. She loved to read because it was as if she could feel the words on the page. To promote this new love, her mother had got her a bean bag chair for her room so she could read in comfort. Elle found no use for such a chair so she sat in the center of her chestnut floor.

    Three years later Elle had painful depression. She couldn't see why it was worth living if nothing came to her easily. It was as if she couldn't see the purpose of life anymore. Perhaps she never learned that life can be hard, but no one told her soon enough. She wanted to end it all, to see all the beautiful parts of life in heaven to answer her dying questions. It wouldn't take much for her to hurt herself since this underlying sadness has lingered in her for ages. One slit was made in her arm with what she grabbed closest to her, the blood slowly crept from that shallow dash and down her pale bruised skin only to trickle onto her beautiful chestnut floor. When it splashed to the floor it was as if a bomb that only she could hear went off. She paused as tears slowly crept from her eyes, then protruding faster than the blood from her wrist. Her poor little room. She frantically went to find where all the blood spilled and in panic tried to wipe it up. She felt it spreading all over. On her wooden floors, her scattered rugs, all over her beautiful little room. With every wipe more came out. She screamed through her tears and hit the floor. Her mother came rushing in. Tears had rolled down her eyes as well but without saying a word she picked Elle up and laid her on her bed, wrapped her little arm up and washed away the blood from the floor and cleaned the white rugs that were now stained red. Elle had soon woke up, her arm still hurting, but she was in the bed that made her happiest. She already lost so much, she knew that she couldn't afford to let depression win. A deep breath was taken and she drifted back to sleep.

The years after this seemed to fly by but even so, the room never changed. The pink and blue walls remained along with the wooden floor that was now stained from her sadness. The furniture remained white and her dolls' eyes were still as beautiful as hers. She had to leave now though, she was grown up. It was time to go. She headed to the door and grabbed her white cane with the red tip on the end and placed her pink sunglasses on.

It was such a beautiful little room...

If only she could see it.

Ж

Do you know the saddest story? One probably popped up when you read that, or maybe a story that isn't even yours danced through your mind.

Were you sad in that story? Or was someone else. Did you give someone something and they didn't give you anything in return? Did someone hurt your feelings and the drama from it all made you sad?

Was it real or pure fiction? How many people are in your sad story? Is it one that lives in your mind or does the world know how sad you were that day. Was it even a day or a span of a few months? Do you look back on it and cry or take a deep breath, relieved that it's over.

Is the chair next to you at dinner suddenly empty every day?

Did you make a decision you never wanted to?

Does someone still call you mommy?

Are you able to still call someone mom.

When you lay your head down at night, do the tears still sting your eyes as the memories overwhelm your head? Has your home turned into a dark reminder of what happened that day? Do you still believe in hope?

When someone reassures you things happen for a reason, does it make you so angry you tell them they're wrong? Do you ask yourself every waking moment, why me? Why did it have to happen to me? What did I do to deserve this? What did we do to deserve this.

Have you ever told yourself never in a million years did I ever think I'd have to endure this? That it would ever happen to me. That all the sudden I'm alone.

You've probably isolated yourself in fear that judgement would make you weaker but in reality, you made yourself weaker by not seeking help. You tell people it's fine but as you sip that coffee with them, you ask yourself why am I here? I just want to go home. You forgot the joy of actually being happy and actually wanting to go out and do something and you just can't stop asking yourself -- Why am I here?

Have you ever written a letter in cursive explaining why you're in pain but you want no one to read it at all? You probably left that

letter on the counter for him to see it but you found yourself coming home an hour later because he never called to see if you were okay. That letter is now crumpled and shoved in a drawer somewhere because you don't want to be here but you just can't do it.
Have you ever felt like that?
Where the world is suddenly small and everything on it no longer matters.
Where time is a construct and everything is man made.
Where you know it'll be alright but your mind just isn't there yet.

    Do you know the saddest story?

A princely character.

This story contains themes of assault.

He was my best friend, my partner in crime, my only friend. I saw him nothing more as my dearest friend but maybe my ignorance ignored his feelings that led him down this path. The world saw him as the man who would never hurt a fly, that flies hurt him. That his crooked smile was somehow genuine and a reflection on how wonderful he was as a person. Often I was asked why I couldn't be more like him and at the time it actually brought me down. To think the world saw him as this unproblematic prince, yet I was the one getting the shit knocked out of me for just being myself. Nothing was ever his fault because lies are just fibs and apparently, that's all I did. It was like screaming into the wind and hoping the breeze from your words would somehow travel to someone to hear your cry for help. Have you ever been slammed onto a foreign bed drugged up against your will. Screaming no until your words slur and you just find yourself crying because they got you at your weakest. Not remembering how you got there and worrying how you'll get home. Trying to kick and punch but your limbs are suddenly cement. Whispering why over and over again and after it's all over you just laid there until it wore off. You laid there trying to reason. You laid there until you convinced yourself it was just a nightmare.

You come home late and when your mother asks where you've been you just smile and say the movies. Yeah, the movies, because it was just a dream. It dies with you because the few breaths for help that came out were silenced. You're the bitch for cutting ties. Why aren't you friends anymore?

    But he's still the prince right?

CARROLLWOOD

Carollwood was a strange town. A town that you never seemed able to escape from once you were there. The odd thing about this little town is that life there was dull and so were the people. Everyone lived as if they were in a single file line. Even the trees stood still most days because not even the wind moved. There was one part of this little town though that was unlike the rest -- Carollwood beach.

1888 was the year I turned thirteen. I went from the big city of Winchester, England to the uneventful Carrollwood, France since my daddy had yet another new job. There weren't many children in Carrollwood. In fact, I thought it was just me. That was until I met a very peculiar boy. He looked around the age of sixteen and had hair as dark as coal along with ghostly pale skin that would blind you if you stared too long. His eyes? I'd assume they're blue but he never looks you in the eye and when he did his chaotic hair covered them. He seemed instantly attracted to me but that may be simply because we were the only two who can repopulate in this godforsaken town. The boy gave me a double take when our eyes did first lock. I suppose he's never seen another female for that matter as well.

"You're new here!" he stated to me.

"Well tha-"

Before I could even finish my sentence he cut me off.

"Come on! I gotta show you something… This may seem forward ma'am but I never met another chillin before!" He exclaimed as he took me by the wrist.

That's when I first saw it. Carolwood beach. It was so unlike the rest of the town. The wind played with my hair gently as the sun illuminated the sand below my feet. There was the sound of joy from the mother bird up in the trees and when the waves hugged my ankles I could feel my eyes watering from pure bliss. I didn't say much. I wasn't sure if I was in awe of the beauty in front of me or still stunned by the audacity that he grabbed me.

"This is beautiful an' all but why did you take me here?" I asked disgruntled.

"Just wait" the boy said with a smirk.

We sat in the warm sand and watched as the ocean conformed making a new painting to admire by the second. Moments later from the distance a man gracefully rose from the ocean on a horse and carriage. I couldn't see a face, or any detail for the matter, since he seemed to be nothing more than a black figure in the distance as his carriage shadowed him. The boy ran knees deep into the ocean to greet the man as the carriage began to slow. I couldn't hear what they were talking about. The boy turned and pointed to me while the man looked my way as he handed him a little silk bag. They gave each other a quick yet stern nod and the man rode back into the ocean. The carriage departed and the boy ran back to shore trying not to shake the bag around too much.

"W-what just happened...who wa-."

"His name's the Giver", the boy said, cutting me off again.

He sat next to me all cozy and I could feel my blood rushing as he began to open the bag. He gently shook out five silver coins and took out a little pink rose in which he bashfully handed to me. There was a moment of silence as I admired the rose with the waves crashing behind me. Pink roses were my favorite.

"Oh god darn!" The boy said frustrated "I don't think I've ever introduced myself! The name's Nick" He said with a sincere yet a goofy smile.

"Lydia…" I said a bit hesitant.

"What a beautiful name!" Nick swiftly responded.

"Huh?" My eyes widened as my cheeks heated up.

"I'm sorry my lady, did I offend you?" He asked concerned.

"N-no… I've just never been told that before."

It was strange how fast the rest of that day went. Before I knew it, the sun was going down and I had spoken to Nick for several hours but it only felt like five. From that day on, Carrollwood seemed less boring, as if the whole town was gray and he was the only color in it. Days turned into months, and months into years, and every afternoon at two the Giver arrived at the shore. Nick once told me as long as you think like a child he'll come. It wasn't until then I realized the Giver only helped people who were unfortunate. Nick came from an abusive family while mine was neglectful. In a way, we were miserable but together we were at peace.

    I was turning seventeen that year, Nick finally proposed to me. The day of my eighteenth birthday, we married. It was a simple wedding to those who attended but it was everything I've dreamt of, simply because he was going to be my husband. Growing up, we dreamt of leaving Carollwood but for some reason, we were always here for many more years to come. Months after we married, the Giver started appearing less frequently. I never dared to go near the shore to meet him. Instead I just watched on the beach as Nick thanked him for the blessings. Years following, the Giver stopped coming completely. It may have been because there were bills to pay and children to tend to, and sometimes we lost hope. Even so, we had each other and every morning we sat at the breakfast table mostly appreciating one another as there was no news around the town. As the afternoon approached, we sat in the sand and looked to the horizon even though we knew he wasn't coming; there was still no place I wanted to be besides sitting in the sand with my Husband.

My worst nightmare became a reality that following year. Nick got out of bed less and less and his soft pale skin turned to a papery gray. The children were married and well off in their new homes, and it was just Nick and I again. I sat by his bedside and watched over him. His eyes really were blue but most likely brighter than they are now as the color started to diminish. A part of me was afraid to wake up every morning, in fear that I'd lose the only one I ever loved. I found the strength to wait on the shore in hopes that the man in the carriage could help in some way, but he never came. As the months went on, a part of me knew it was coming, but I refused to let go. I woke up as I did every morning to set the table -- only this time, he never woke up. I gently shook him in hopes that he was just having another bad day but his body was freezing and that of a rag doll. In my devastation I was in complete silence before screaming in agony. My tears puddled his shirt as I curled up holding him as I knew it would be the last time. For hours I laid there crying until I fell asleep. Breakfast went cold.

    It never got easier when my husband passed. My once beautiful home was now a cluttered mess. My children would often visit but when they went home I was alone again. Every morning I still set the table for two in hopes he would somehow join me again, but instead I seldomly ate as I stared at the empty chair across from me. As a little girl who grew up alone I thought I'd never have to endure that again when he touched my life. It was never the same as most my days were spent sobbing.

    I went to the Carolwood beach, just as we always did. Only this time, I sat in the cold sand alone. There he was. The Giver came to shore and I felt something for the first time in a while as I lifted my dress to go knees deep into the icy cold ocean. There I waited as the carriage came to a stop. His face was more apparent now and his smile was kind. Just as the first syllable was to escape my lips to thank him he greeted me with "Don't worry. I'll take good care of Nick." The warmth of my tears streamed down my face as I heard my husband's name for the first time in years. The Giver gently leaned down and grabbed my hand, placing a small silk bag in my now papery palms. I opened it in front of him and inside was neither silver nor roses, it was a little sheet of paper.

"My dearest Lydia. It's okay to be happy. I'll be right here when the time comes but for now try to enjoy yourself. I love you."

As the carriage began to move it passed my teary face. In the carriage was Nick with a bright smile and looking youthful as ever. The man was right.

Nick will be just fine.

To my ignorance

This story contains strong language.

How did I not expect this, is any man really perfect? After all, most never grow up until their thirties. You'd think there's only room for one cheatfull and toxic relationship in your lifetime but that's only what those quotes in Vogue want you to believe. To say I have no fault would be a lie but it's mostly in harm to myself not others. Every time I try to wrap my head around it I feel nauseous and enraged. That son of a bitch thinks he could string me along and get away with it. It's a good thing he doesn't know the intel I do. When I asked him what he did that morning he replied with a sheepish "not much" as he couldn't even look me in the eye. I guess it was opposite day because his "not much" was a whole lot. I played it cool even though my ears were bleeding from anger and my fist clenched by the audacity. He really thinks he could do something like that and get away with it.

I gave him a second chance by asking what he had for breakfast after I left for work. A brief pause draped the room as he calculated "Uh eggs." We don't have eggs and haven't had eggs in weeks. "Really, eggs?" I questioned. You could almost feel the heat radiating from his face since he knew the deep shit he was in. I closed my eyes preparing for the worst. "Just tell me the truth". Another pause nearly choked me as the room was ringing and my heart pulsing. "I watch porn" he said quietly. I almost wanted to laugh as he believed it to be some crime so expecting to hear something along the lines of Pornhub I asked "and where do you watch it?". "Instagram…." he confessed. I began to laugh as it dawned on me that Instagram doesn't allow porn. In protest I demanded his phone and only one girl popped up on the screen. The worst part, she looked similar to me. How moronic do you have to be. Upon further interrogation I discovered they knew each other in person. Confused after seeing his empty DM box he informed me that he has no direct contact with her, he just simply follows her. After putting two and two together I realized this chick has no idea he still exists let alone knew creeps were using her photos for unethical purposes.

I don't remember much after that then slamming his sorry ass into the wall and chucking his phone so far it's probably in Mars right now. It was so incredibly stupid that for some reason the first person I called was my boss. I'm not sure why, maybe since she reflected my mom so much I felt like it was a preview for what's to come before I had to inform my mother. She was the only calm aspect of that day and gave me the next day off after I informed her "I feel like I'm going to fucking kill him right now" but I digress.

There were so many fragile decisions to come after this whole ordeal on who to call next to vent to and that's when it hit me. His mother. Now I'm not sure how I didn't have her number in the seven years we were together but I marched back inside and handed my phone to him. "Dial your mother's number."

"Huh?"

"You heard me, dial your mother's number."

Reluctant he dialed it into my phone. It rang and at that moment the anger manifested to a point where I just came to a standstill. I figured this is where I'd get my satisfaction but it was far from it. Right as I'm telling her what happened she interrupted me.

"But they all do that."

"Excuse me?"

"All boys masturbate to porn he did nothing wrong."

"I'd agree with you except it wasn't porn, it was a girl he knew."

"Well I'm sorry you're sad. Sorry to change the subject but are we still celebrating his birthday this year?"

At that moment I wasn't sure what pissed me off more, him or his mother. Then I sat and asked myself, am I the crazy one? The reassurance came when I called my mother, and that's when I knew I wasn't the nut job here. She flew over faster than a panther chasing its prey. I sat on the couch as she ripped him a new one on my behalf, in a way I was a little impressed as he didn't say a word or move an inch. My mom was the only one on my side as it appears the rest of the world lowered their standards on what to expect out of a relationship.

 I filled my backpack with just the essentials and anything of value just in case I came home and the house was empty. To really make it sting I grabbed our beloved guinea pig on the way out so he would truly be alone. I was planning out every revenge scheme and how I would make him pay until the phone rang. It was his father, in other words the only good man left on this earth. He told me he heard the news and how sorry he was. I reassured him, it wasn't his fault, just his son's. He continued to tell me he will ensure nothing like this would ever happen again and his son is going to pay tenfold. I hung up the phone with a sigh of relief that someone other than blood knew how messed up the situation was, but I had to wonder what he told him. I came home a few days after the incident just to have him turn around. He had a buzz cut and a cake that read "I'm sorry" presented on the table. To my ignorance I bursted out laughing and gave him a hug.

    Maybe I'm the dumbass.

A second chance

Of course I love my husband. If I didn't, why would I still be married to him? Of course things as of late have been a tad rocky to say the least. We don't spend as much time together anymore so I took it as an opportunity to improve myself. Currently, I'm the breadwinner for the house. I come home every night from work and there he is wasting away on the couch, indulging in lethal food and brain numbing video games. I began to realize it may be me at fault for not trying to engage in change to fix our marriage. For months I would come home to that sight and just march right to the bedroom to pass out, since being a nurse takes more than enough out of a person. In all these months of pondering and wondering, not once has he made the effort to change either. So when his mother wishes "things would have been different" I laugh to myself at the thought that she thinks her son is a prize to be won. I still love my husband though. The dishes are still dirty when I come home late at night and the clothes unwashed, I can't be the only woman who would be upset by this. Not once has he actually done anything nice for me either to say the least. Even a simple "I missed you" when I came through the door would have been enough for me. So I got my schedule changed and now come home in the afternoon, in which he is still a bum all day. Call it lack of communication but is it really when you've said it so many times? I still love my husband though. I wanted things to go back to how they used to be and I figured him not working was probably what caused him to bum out. He's a very smart man, so I knew any job he'd apply for would eat him right up. I was right, as always, he was hired on the spot. So all excited, I couldn't wait to come home to ask how his first day of work was, but he wasn't there. I called him, his workplace, and his mother, but nothing -- not even an idea of where he went. Then I turned on the news. He was shot. I was shocked to say the least

        But of course I love my husband.

How criminal

Just a small following, who cares. I only opened the stupid account because my friends are on it. I like watching the random videos and the mindless distraction it gives me from everyday life. I always wondered what would happen if I posted something of my own. Would anyone ever see it? It's okay if they don't. I'm more of a lurker not a creator. Here goes nothing. Just as I thought, it's been seven hours and not a view. Off to work I go just to fall in the same cycle when I return. Three thousand notifications? How could this be? I guess I could be a creator if I tried. Here goes another one, and another one. The numbers are piling up and by the day I'm climbing the ladder, the people love me. Famous creators are following me and I feel like I found a purpose in my content. Even though I get no more than twenty likes a video I still am happy to create. If only it could take off like some but that's okay, it's all just for fun anyways. Time to post some more and more. The numbers are slowing down but I'm sure it's just an off day for me on the site. I'm so close to my goal but it seems it came to a stand still. I don't understand why my talent is going unnoticed. I've spent hours on my video and you would think more people would see it. What do they have that I don't? I'll just put on a little more makeup and try a new style, that seems to be the trend. My content isn't working so let me try something new, a little out of my comfort zone but it's bound to get me to the top. Let me post more and more until my eyes hurt and my voice cracks. Oh look, she posted a new video, let's see the competition. That's. . my video and she has. . . ten thousand likes. . .I only have twenty.

      How criminal. I quit.

A best friend

Janice was a normal girl, who lived a pretty average life. She never bothered her parents for much, except a puppy -- a common dream among many seven year old girls. After months of begging, her parents gave in. Welcomed into the family was a little black lab. She was a strong little thing with ears that flopped over her eyes and paws the size of quarters. She was presented to Janice with a little pink bow gently wrapped around her neck and a collar that read "Lucy". In pure excitement Janice hugged Lucy tight and started to cry as she looked forward to the fun she'd have with her new friend.

    Janice was an only child, but managed to find ways to entertain herself when alone. Hard work was not foreign to her as her chores entailed scrubbing the tile cracks and disinfecting the toilets. Taking care of a puppy was easy, or so she thought. After filling her bowl in the morning she'd scope the house for any accidents, which there almost always was. After mopping up the urine and discarding the dung she'd open the patio door to allow Lucy play time. Lucy would run in circles and roll till her heart was content then she would just lay in the grass and stare at Janice panting. Together, they'd go back inside where Lucy would slurp up every last drop of water in her bowl. Janice found such joy taking care of Lucy, but even so she was exhausted by the middle of the day. Lucky for her Lucy was a good girl.

    As Lucy grew, every night before bed she'd lay her head on the edge of Janice's bed. They'd look each other in the eyes until Janice fell asleep. Janice loved her parents but even so, the amount of love she had for Lucy outweighed all others. It was something she'd never say out loud but she knew Lucy was the only one who genuinely cared for her. Her father never gave so much as a glance to her when he got home and her mother was never sober enough to remember who Janice was. She couldn't hold it against them as their living arrangement wasn't the most ideal, but she knew at least Lucy loved her and that's all she needed to stay chipper.

Some would say Janice was lucky since she was able to do school online but if only they knew why. Not even Janice herself knew why she was too weak to walk the halls with the other children. It didn't matter to her though since it only meant that she got to spend more time with Lucy throughout the day. Wherever she went Lucy would follow. She'd look down and there she'd be sleeping at her toes. Janice never talked to herself but when she did it was often her whispering "I love my Lucy" as she gazed at her. Even though Lucy couldn't understand, she knew how much she was loved and would just embrace every moment of it. It was always like this from the moment they met.

As the years flew by both Janice and Lucy slowed down. It became harder for Janice to leave the bed and would often lay there most the day trying to keep up with her schoolwork. Lucy stopped rolling in the grass and only could finish half her food but her heart never changed. Even if it was hard to lift her head her little face was always on the edge of the bed waiting to be kissed. Janice took breaks more frequently to appreciate Lucy and always found herself falling asleep with her hand on her now boney face. The following week, Janice had some trouble breathing but it never dimmed her optimistic personality.

One day in the late spring Janice laid there in her bed with the window cracked letting in that comforting breeze and listened to the trees shaking, which felt like hellos. She stared out to watch the clouds in hopes that maybe it could make her feel better. Her mother came in and gently rubbed Jancie's pale face. Tears quietly traced her face as she knew she was in part to blame for this outcome. With every ounce of strength, Janice turned her head and whispered "I want my Lucy." The door cracked open and in came Lucy as her tail slowly swifted side to side and her ears drooped beyond her face. Janice smiled the best she could as she slowly moved her hand to the edge of the bed. Lucy placed her face under her hand and began to whimper. Petting her as their eyes locked Janice softly whispered "You know you're my best friend forever right." The petting slowed down as Janice closed her eyes for the last time but Lucy didn't leave her side.

For months after Lucy laid next to Jancie's empty bed. One morning Janice's mother heard a giggle coming from her old room and when the door opened, there was Lucy laying on Janice's bed, laid to rest. They were finally together again. Now that's true love.

Ghosted

This story has elements of suicide.

Every year Emma's family would go on a road trip up north for the Holidays. It wasn't her favorite outing as she much rather be in her room jamming out to bands that probably won't be around next year. Still, she figured it did no harm in spending time with her family every once in a while. The drive usually took about twelve hours, so Emma and her brother were asleep for most of it. She popped in her headphones and let her mind wander as she daydreamed out the window. She felt her eyelids get heavy as her head drifted to being gently squished on the window. It was a bumpy road, but she didn't feel a thing.

When her eyes opened she found herself laying on her bed. Confused, she wandered around trying to find her family, but the house was empty. Frantically, she tried calling her mother, but her phone was nowhere to be found. So Emma waited, and waited until the days began blending into each other. The front door finally opened and in walked her Mother, Father, and younger Brother. In excitement she jolted out of her room to greet them but came to a hault when she got a good look at them all. Her mother was hysterically crying as her father had his arms wrapped around her black sweater. Her brother's eyes were red and he too was in all black but covered in bandages and bruises. Emma gasped as she tried asking them what happened but the commotion over took her words and she never got her answer. She wasn't sure how but she knew it must have been something horrendous as her mother never cries.

When the new semester started up Emma hopped on the bus as she always did only this time her friends gave her the cold shoulder. To say Emma was baffled would be an understatement as she didn't know what she may have done wrong. Emma was never a fan of school, actually, she despised it with every fiber of her being. She went to the front office in hopes to figure out why she didn't receive her schedule in the mail but they refused to help her. In frustration, Emma marched out of the office and made her way home. In the past, when she skipped school, the officers would stop and question where she was going and her reasoning, but this time, not a word as she walked right on by.

  When she arrived home she announced herself but still no response. All she could hear was the silent weeping from her mother's room. Emma's mother hasn't left her room in weeks and it was evident by how disgusting the house was becoming. Emma tried her best to help around the house with chores but she always felt like no matter how hard she tried things were never clean enough for her liking. At this point, it was going on for months. Her father would come home and when she came out to greet him, he only did so much as sigh as he made his way to the bedroom. When Emma's younger brother came home he always looked beat and went to waste away at the computer for hours. With still no luck in finding her phone, Emma truly felt alone. Oftentimes, when she'd look out the window, she'd see her friends talking to her mom and not even so much as ask to see her. When Emma would come back from her daily strolls she'd notice little by little her room was being cleared out. She confronted her mother but all she could do was cry and cry in Emma's face.

    Since then her room has been completely cleared out and the rage Emma has stored for now what felt years has turned to a dark depression.

She never felt when she hurt herself anymore as the only pain consumed her mind. She left a note describing her grievance in hopes that her family would finally understand the pain they've put her through. She snuck into her father's shed and stole a rope. Upon entering her bedroom with tears in her eyes she pushed the boxes left in her room underneath the ceiling fan, where she then began to tie the noose. Just as she was about to climb the box to her demise, her mother popped in and laid on Emma's bed. Before Emma could turn to her mother, she's already begun sobbing on the bed. Emma warned her mother she was going to do it if she didn't start noticing her again. Her mother didn't respond. In anger, Emma climbed the old dusty boxes and put her head through the loop. "Mom, I'm serious, I'm going to do it," Emma cried. Again, no answer. Out of exasperation, Emma kicked the boxes from underneath her to where she fell through the rope and landed on the carpeted floor. She looked up in horror at her sobbing mother, and in her hand, was a picture of Emma and the day she died. Emma had been dead for two months.

Grandma's house

The summers at my grandmother's house were some of the best. Her beige carpets would turn into the sand as the blue sheets were the ocean. When we were exhausted from crashing the waves and camping out in our pillow forts, my grandmother would ring the bell and like little mice, we'd run to the dinner table. Everything was in a bowl, even down to the fruit cups. She'd often make a meal that was so delicious it became a signature at her house. That meal was Shrimp and Shells. As an Italian family, you're probably expecting some fancy sauce or the best shrimp money can buy, but in fact it was simply just pasta and frozen shrimp left to thaw. It was because grandma made it why it was so special.

    After dinner, my sister was old enough to use the shower, while my brother and I were placed in a bubble bath of every child's dreams. Like little ducks, she'd take us out one by one and shake us dry. My brother was free to go before me as his short hair dried in minutes. I, on the other hand, sat on my great grandmother's chair as my grandma brushed and dried me to a fluff. We'd put on our mismatched pajamas and peeked our eyes over the counter as grandma popped popcorn with no butter or salt. Together we'd sit in the living room and watch whatever the first movie was to pop up. As the night quickly came to an end, she'd tuck us into bed and tell us stories about a mermaid who befriends a giant bunny, or a dragon protecting his village. All I knew was that she gave us the best time a child could ask for.

    The year my grandfather passed away was not an easy one. My siblings and I sat in Wendy's playing with the just-released Over the Hedge toys when my mother had a panic attack. Due to its severity, she was hospitalized as my siblings and I were sent to my grandmother's house. I remember looking out the window most the day, waiting for my mother to come home and wondering if grandpa was with her. I asked my grandmother where they'd gone and she told me that mommy would be home soon but grandpa would be away a little longer since he went on vacation. At the time, I pictured my grandfather in a Hawaiian shirt and silly flip flops but months started to pass and he never came home. We weren't told right away as my other grandfather passed away shortly before and it would have been a lot for a child to process at once. When the time came and they had to tell me, I was told he went to heaven. I wasn't sure what it meant but I assumed it was some sort of beach island as my grandfather loved to sail. I'd find myself crying a lot and that's when my grandmother told me Heaven can look like whatever I wanted it to, that whatever is my happy place is what Heaven will be. I still live with that as a strange comfort -- that there's something out there but if you ask me, I don't think my grandfather ever left her side.

In the summer of fifth grade, we moved closer to my grandmother. It was a peace of mind knowing that she was no more than fifteen minutes away. We'd visit her every Wednesday and stayed over on the weekends. Time always went slower at grandma's house but it never bothered me. I would just sit and appreciate how blessed I was to still have a grandma. A lot of people like to label themselves as "kind", but my grandmother never needed to say how much she did for others because she always just quietly did it. It's not every day you meet a selfless woman, one who would give you her last shirt if it meant she could help. When the new school year started, mentally, I was in a bad spot and the words I spoke to others weren't the kindest. Why I said those things still haunts me as it wasn't in my nature to be mean. When my grandmother found out she sat me in the rocking chair and kneeled down. Not an ounce of anger came out of her voice when she asked me why I was being mean. I wasn't sure what to say. I just remember crying in which she said to me "I'm disappointed in you not because I think you're a bad person but because I've always told you how you treat people changes the world so why did you choose those words?" Even after what's been close to ten years, I still remember those words like it was yesterday. Since then, I never spoke an ill word again to others.

    For some reason, my grandmother didn't have bandages or paper towels. We're not really sure why, but it was always interesting to see what she chose to use in their place. I remember my dear friend got a cut on her hand and in panic we searched the drawers to find a bandage, after no luck we bit the bullet and told grandma. My grandmother came back with a menstrual pad and a few rubber bands then began to wrap it around my friends hand. To my surprise, she just laughed and thanked grandma, reminding her how much she loved her. Throughout my awkward middle school phase, I remember showing my grandmother "Black Butler" and years after that she'd called me Ciel, no matter who I dressed up as. She would watch anything you showed her and even though she most likely didn't understand a lot of it, she always did it for us.

    A favorite story she'd tell us is the one about how she met my grandfather. Back in the day my grandmother was, to put it plainly, really hot. She told me how back then, you went out in a group of friends and it was almost like a double date. She was seeing this boy often from her school but they would just go on dates nothing really serious. A friend of hers wanted to set her up on a blind date. My grandmother laughed and refused but after months of being worn down she said yes to get it over with. That's when she met my grandfather. She tells me they went to see a movie but doesn't remember the actual film itself, since they talked through the entire thing. She always says she knew it the moment she met him -- that would be her husband. They dated as well for a while and she would still occasionally see the other boy. That's when my grandfather said "Marilyn, what are we doing here. You have to choose." So the very next day, my grandmother met up with the other boy, to whom she said "I'm sorry. I choose Jack." The rest was history. On her nineteenth birthday, my grandfather proposed and they were married six months later.

I learned of many tales how amazing my grandfather was as a husband. In Italian households, it was frowned upon to have your partner spend the night. One chilly New York afternoon, before my grandparents were married, my grandfather got sick. He took a train about an hour between cities to see my grandma every weekend, so it wasn't a quick trip. He laid on the couch and when the sunset, my great grandmother asked him to leave. My grandmother begged her not to let him travel sick in the snow but it wasn't up for debate, he had to go. They bundled him up and sent him off with that night's dinner and on the train he went home. My grandmother always says to me "and that poor man had to travel through all that with a stuffy nose." My grandmother was truly a princess growing up as she didn't do so much as lift a finger, as most Italian girls in my family were raised. Their first night as a married couple, my grandmother attempted to make pasta for the first time. She laughs when she tells me how she didn't let the water boil before pouring it in and it was hard as a rock when she served it. Even so, my grandfather ate every last bite as my grandmother attempted to take the bowl away from him in embarrassment. My grandmother always told my sister and me growing up that there was no need to learn how to cook; we'll just know how to do it when the time comes...but that story reminds us otherwise.

High School was a rough time for me but that's a tale on its own. Grandma was never the touchy feely type who'd ask you what's wrong, instead she gave it to you bluntly. One morning before school, I was sobbing at the breakfast table as I did every morning. She asked me why I was crying as she handed me some pancakes in a bowl. "Today is a bad day," I told her. "But today didn't even start yet." I sighed through my tears with a "I know, but every day is a bad day". That's when she told me something that still lives in my mind. "Before your eyes open and your feet touch the floor, tell yourself today will be a good day and it will be." She was right, even though emotions can't be flipped like a switch. From then on, my days were always better if that's how my morning started. Things were still rough but I was thankful to have my grandma and mother as moral support through it all.

    I began making videos and she was the star in any she was in. Her kindness radiated through the screen and everyone she met just loved her so much. No matter how many hats I'd put on a day, she never thought it was crazy. With every new interest and every last hobby, you could always find her sitting on the couch smiling as she watched me create. When we watched Hallmark movies, I'd point to the girl handing the main character her coffee and say "Look grandma! I'm going to be her someday!" She always assured me I would be and how my name would be all over her television someday. It was a silly dream but something I eagerly worked for to make it come true for my grandmother. Grandma's house was the creative sanctuary where no dream was too big and no talent unnoticed.

    At the end of highschool, I introduced my now husband to her. My grandmother loved all my friends but something about my husband made her heart soft. She was never one to tell us what to do or who to be with but the night he left she told me it was meant to be. In months that he lost his job she opened her doors for him to stay, which was a big deal as it wasn't something we do in our family. The day I knew she loved him was when he was allowed into her bedroom to use the restroom, no one ever went into her bedroom regardless of the reason. The day he proposed to me wasn't only the happiest day of my life, but hers as well. She always saw him as one of her grandchildren but now she knew he'd never leave. When he found work I moved with him about two hours away, but even so we still visited almost every weekend. Every time that door opened, we rejoiced as we all got to be together again. This went on for about a year and a half until the Coronavirus pandemic caused my husband to lose his job again.

    By the grace of God, his next job was much closer to my family. We continued to plan the wedding but during those months of unemployment, we eloped. The day of my bridal shower my grandmother looked so happy and was enjoying every moment of it. My friends were able to see her again for what would probably be the last time and we were surrounded by family we hadn't seen in years. We already knew grandma most likely couldn't make it to the rehearsal dinner and neither could my father since it was a lot for them, but what we didn't know is that my grandmother wasn't going to be at the wedding.

    The week of my wedding, my grandmother was in the hospital. At the time, we didn't know how or what caused her sudden collapse. In the middle of the night she escaped the hospital, gown and all, while calling a cab. She let herself in around five in the morning while we slept. It wasn't until my brother came rushing into the room to inform my mother and I that grandma was sitting on the couch. We genuinely thought she was a ghost by how badly she scared us. She said to me she wasn't missing my wedding for nothing and that she'd go back to the hospital after the wedding. Hysterical, a part of me wanted to cancel everything but I feared it may be the only time my grandmother could see me in my dress. The day of the rehearsal came and my mother called to inform me that at that moment of time, grandma was not able to make it to the wedding. I was upset, not because I wanted her to be there, but because my grandma has never been too weak to go anywhere. The morning of my wedding came and it was certain that she wouldn't be strong enough to make it. When she spoke to me she said "don't you cry, you have a beautiful day. I can't wait to see the pictures of how beautiful you are." For her sake I knew the show must go on. I couldn't tell you how I didn't cry all day, my shock probably prevented it. The wedding came to a close and my mother asked if I needed help getting out of my dress, I informed her there was one last stop I needed to make before the dress came off. I squished into the car as we pulled up to my grandmother's house. I rang her doorbell and saw her in the hallway for what will probably be the last time. Barely standing on her own, she reached out to tell me how beautiful I looked. I was reluctant to leave that night, as a part of me wasn't sure what the weeks to come would entail. I just always thought she would be there every weekend.

What started as an infection turned out to be stage four cancer. I'm not sure how this ended up in God's plan for her but I never believed this hellish nightmare could come true. The worst part is there's no conclusion yet. As I write this now, on my grandfather's birthday, I ask myself why life is so cruel to the kindest people. I know however this ends up someone will be waiting for her on either side. I'm grateful to have had a grandmother longer than most but I'm selfish and always wanted her to be here much longer. We still visit her house to keep things in order but the only difference is, when the door opens, she's not there waiting anymore. I want nothing more than to hear that bell ring for dinner and we all sit down again, as a family.

Poems

Cold Showers

I take cold showers.

Does anyone really want to?

Sometimes no matter how much you turn the knob it's still cold.

It's not so bad once you've done it for so long.

There's many worse things than a cold shower.

Why I still cry every time is unknown,

But just like the knob no matter how much I turn,

My emotions don't change.

Would I even feel better if the water was warm,

Or would it just scald me and make me never want to shower again.

Even if I was trapped in a cube of ice at least I know what the cold feels like.

It's the comfort of knowing my fingers will turn purple,

And my skin will become tight.

That I can expect to turn that knob and cold water will pour out.

Knowing how every day for the rest of my life will be the same,

Whether it be a good or bad day,

A successful or boring one,

One thing will never change,

I take cold showers.

What is tomorrow

Tomorrows never promised,

You may think you're going to the store,

But God has a different plan.

Just when you think you've finally figured it all out,

Something happens to wipe the smile from your face.

You may never see that friend you fought with again

Or they may never see you.

You can dream about the life you'll have,

Until you realize the heart stopped beating.

You think putting it on a calendar will ensure that day will come,

But what if yours stops midyear.

We try to point the finger to ease our minds,

But oftentimes there is no one to blame,

Just nature.

We believe as humans we're entitled to control

But only God has access to the switch.

If you never find the purpose in living,

Take a deep breath and understand how

someone else could.

It could open your eyes or close them

completely,

But choose wisely because,

Tomorrows never promised.

Until we meet again

Until we meet again,

Heaven will treat you well,

The sun will never beat in your face but instead shine upon you.

There will always be flowers and never storms,

I hope you enjoy what Heaven has in store.

You'll see your friends you watched us say goodbye to long ago and they'll never leave again,

You'll never be lonely or afraid anymore,

You're able to run again and bark,

And eat until your heart's content.

You'll be able to see things you haven't been able to for years, and be able to comfort another child's tears.

But,

The only thing that's missing is us,

and even though it seems like forever away,

Enjoy heaven my little friend.

Until we meet again,

You're forever young.

The moon Cries

The moon cries as the clouds dance across its surface.

No one knows why it makes the moon upset,

But all we know is the earth is wet,

From the tears the little moon can't stop shedding,

We try live our daily lives,

But tears are like acid so the world sees our pain

We all cry.

No matter how hard we try,

To conceal it.

It's because it's hard to say goodbye.

On a cold spring day when you went away,

We were told it was only a vacation.

Weeks to years you never came home,

For your spirit roamed the house.

But we did not know.

Yet we still waited for you.

With the pale pink blanket on your chair,

And your side of the bed still made,

In hopes if you do arrive home.

The door will always be open for you.

Six was the age I said goodbye,

But the little girl in me still feels empty.

I never got to hug my grandpa goodbye.

The moon started crying the day you left.

A broken oven

There should be a baby baking in my tummy,

But it's been far too long.

The months of trying,

The years of crying,

It's almost as if everyone else can have one,

Except me.

I know there's more to a woman than the children she bares,

But it's all I've wanted.

To hold a baby girl,

To kiss a baby boy,

To tell them my tales of life,

To ensure theirs will be better than mine.

Every announcement of course I'm happy for them,

But I still sob the moment I get home.

When a mother tells me it was an accident,

When she says she made a mistake,

I just sit and wonder how they got so lucky,

To have a baby baking in their tummy,

And I'm still alone.

If only she knew

She's the only one I call during my break,

My mother that is.

I let her in on my day,

And she tells me hers.

The days she can't talk to me,

I don't take a break at all.

I have no interest in eating in the office,

Or driving off with a coworker.

I rather sit in my car,

With my mom on the phone.

When others get jealous,

I remind them my mother comes first,

And I'm not ashamed in the least to show her off.

It's not an easy job being the best mother in the world,

But yet she makes it look so easy.

To her it's just an hour of the day,

To me it's the best hour of the day.

I look forward to nothing more than it,

That hour that gives me the strength to finish my day,

So when you see me rushing out the door,

Racing to my car,

I really have nowhere to go.

I just sit and wait,

For the phone to ring.

Freedom

I quit my job today,

Something I've never done.

I couldn't help it.

I marched right in there and gave them a piece of my mind.

At least I did in my head.

I was very polite,

Maybe even too polite.

But yet I'm here longer than expected.

Aren't I supposed to say my peace and I'm let free?

I guess I could've walk out,

But it's not in my nature.

I should of yelled in their face like they've done to me,

But what good is that?

There's a time and place for everything,

And those were both today.

Even if it's not how I dreamt,

I'm still free.

And can stay up as long as I want,

I'm a little scared,

But who wouldn't be?

But it finally happened.

I quit my job.

The garden

Something pushed me to the garden today,

I haven't left the house in months,

Not even to take a breath of air.

When the door opened the sun pierced my eyes,

And I could feel my body tense.

But there was a gentle breeze that danced through my hair,

As the clovers hugged my toes,

And the rose bush whistled.

For what hasn't been months I found myself there for hours,

Sitting on my creaking bench watching the clouds sail the sky.

It brought me back to when I was a child,

When my grandmother gently pushed my swing,

As I gleefully giggled looking at a sky that is similar to today.

A reminder that ten years is nothing more than a minute,

And innocence is just a memory.

Even as it grew chill I still sat there,

Trying to hold on to that bliss.

Who knows what trance led me to the garden,

But maybe I needed to go.

To remember how beautiful life can be.

Vows

My grandmother always told me when you meet the right one you'll know.
I never knew what she meant until I held you for the first time.
There are so many but still not enough words to describe how amazing of a man you are.
You've seen me at my best and stuck by me at my worst.

You cheer me on when others have given up and brought the daylight back in my head when it's gotten dark.

You've never made me feel wrong even when I was.

When I asked God to find peace, shortly after I met you.

You remind me everyday how a man should be because you make me feel like a queen.

It feels like just yesterday we met because everyday with you sails by so fast and someday when my hands wrinkle and they're still holding your face, I want you to know that you have given me the time of my life simply because I love you.
Till death due us part won't apply to us because you'll always be my husband

in this life and every

after.

To my grandmother

A blanket of depression wrapped my

shoulders,

And I try to tell myself it'll pass,

But she said cancer.

Why did it have to be cancer?

I play it off as everything is fine,

But I haven't touched a spoon in days,

Or washed the ones that have moved into the

sink for weeks.

It towers over me as I wait for it to collapse.

Her heart is gold but her head is hard,

But if she can't do it, who could.

I'm afraid to wake up and hear the news,

And like a coward afraid to call.

She's so loved that no matter which side she

passes,

Many loved ones will wait with open arms.

It's hard to fathom the thought of her leaving,

But at least I know my grandfather waits there

at the gate,

To show her around her new paradise.

It's selfish of me to pray she stays in her

current one,

She's just that amazing though.

That life would never be the same,

And the sun would stop rising.

So grandma if you ever read this in print or

heaven,

Just know I love you more than any poem can

depict,

And you be sure to tell them,

Heavy on the rum.

Words of wisdom from my grandmother.

"When you open your eyes in the morning and before your toes hit the floor, tell yourself today will be a good day and it will be."

"Heaven will look like anything you want it to. Wherever you're happiest is what heaven will look like for you."

"I'm disappointed in you not because I think you're a bad person but because I've always told you how you treat people changes the world so why did you choose those words?"

"When you walk around school give a smile to the other kids, because chances are they'll smile too and you never know you may make their day"

"That kid can do anything just like her mother. I can see it now, Hunter Blaise fashion line!"

"It's the changing of the plates!"

"Did you take your vitamins?"

"When you meet them you know, what's the use in messing around?"

"Just be kind. That's all there is to it,

is to just be kind."

A NOTE FROM THE AUTHOR.

I hope you enjoyed my first collection of short stories. These stories have been written throughout different periods of my life and are based on very real experiences. My darkest days have kept these stories in the archives but due to recent events, I realized there's nothing to be afraid of anymore and how these stories may help someone who is having a bad day. My grandmother is my best friend and is the main reason why I wanted to publish a book and the shortness of it. As of January 6th 2021, my grandmother has cancer and the outcome is yet foreseen. She always told me she wanted to see my name everywhere someday before she passed, and now that someday is closer than we ever prayed it would be, all I can do is make her proud with what I have. A lot of these stories were written off the principle of how volatile life can be, and you never know where it can throw you. I lost my grandfathers at a young age and I hold a lot of resentment against myself for not doing more. Grief is a common concept in my writing as it never goes away. There are days where my mind is free, and others where I'm back sitting on the edge of the bathtub when my mother tells me the news. That was the first time I experienced grief, and even though there is nothing I can do to change whom life has taken away from me, I can always be with them again in my writing. When not grief, I find myself writing when my depression consumes me. I am legally blind and lose more eyesight by the year. It's something I wouldn't wish on my worst enemy, but instead of wasting the last years I can see crying, I found a way to turn this fear into acceptance knowing that many blind people live fulfilling lives. These stories aren't meant to ruin your day or make you be sad; The intention is to make you discover what life means to you and even if you don't always win, someone out there already knows your story but in a different context. Whether you never found help or lost someone you love, your emotions take over or acceptance isn't there yet, I want you to know someone is listening. Never think your feelings are invalid because someone has it worse. If it means something to you then it's valid. It's okay to do nothing sometimes. If you got out of bed today, that's already something. With time you'll find your peace, just take it slow.

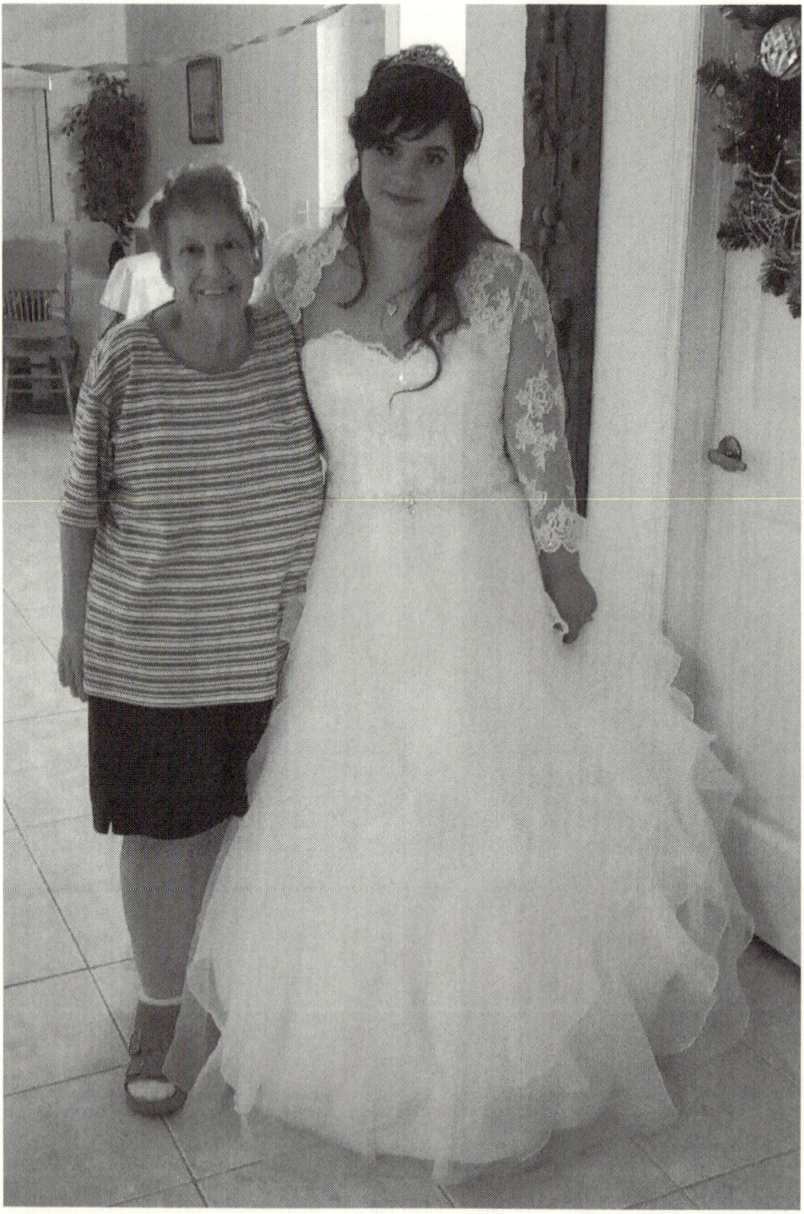

Made in the USA
Monee, IL
21 January 2021